39 Kids on th
The
Best Friends
Club

Look for these and other books
in the **39 Kids on the Block** series:

#1 *The Green Ghost of Appleville*

#2 *The Best Present Ever*

#3 *Roses Are Pink and You Stink!*

#4 *The Best Friends Club*

#5 *Chicken Pox Strikes Again*

39 Kids on the Block

The Best Friends Club

by Jean Marzollo
illustrations by Irene Trivas

SCHOLASTIC INC.
New York Toronto London Auckland Sydney

Grateful acknowledgement is made for permission to use three riddles from Grizzly Riddles *by Katy Hall and Lisa Eisenberg. Text copyright © 1989 by Katy Hall and Lisa Eisenberg. Reprinted by permission of the publisher, Dial Books for Young Readers.*

ISBN 0-590-42726-1

12 11 10 9 8 7 6 5 4 1 2 3 4 5/9

Printed in the U.S.A. 40

First Scholastic printing, April 1990

For "Panchita"
Francisca S. Villarreal
of Brownsville, Texas.

With special thanks to Jeff, John,
Crysten, Michael, Lee, Ashley,
Jason, Richard, Robb, Jenny H.,
Jonathan, Tanya, Courtney, Zach,
Melanie, Jenny T., Sydney, Corey,
and their second-grade teacher
Mrs. Liberty, and to
Dr. Olivia Saracho, professor of
education at the University
of Maryland.
—J.M.

To Frost.
—I.T.

Thirty-nine kids live on Baldwin Street.
They range in age from babies to teenagers.
The main kids in this story are:
Maria Lopez,
Mary Kate Adams,
Michael Finn,
Rusty Morelli,
Jane Fox,
John Beane,
Lisa Wu,
Joey Adams,
Fizz Eddie Fox

SPY STREET
RUSTY MORELLI
APPLE APARTMENTS
APPLE APARTMENTS
KIMBERLY
MARY KATE and JOEY
FIZZ EDDIE and JANE
1.
3.
5.
7.
9.
15.
17.
19
21
ORCHARD STREET
APPLEVILLE SCHOOL
BALDWIN STREET
MAIN STREET
4
6
8
10
12
14
RESTAURANT
JOHN BEANE
MICHAEL FINN
MARIA LOPEZ
LISA WU
CORTLAND STREET

Chapter 1

Tuesday morning Mr. Carson stopped silent reading early.

"Today is April first," he said.

Maria Lopez was smiling to herself. She was reading *Grizzly Riddles.* The last riddle she read was:

Why did the grizzly cross the road?

Because it was the chicken's day off.

Now Maria closed her book. She wondered why Mr. Carson had cut reading time short.

Maybe he wanted the April calendar done right away. This made Maria nervous.

Should she volunteer to do it?

She hadn't done one yet.

Half of her wanted to do it. But the other half was shy.

To change the calendar, first you erased the chalk writing for the old month. That left empty calendar lines on the board. These lines didn't erase.

Next you wiped the lines with a damp rag. That left the calendar clean and empty.

Then you wrote special days coming up in the new month.

Maria had always wanted to write on the board. But there was one problem. To do so, she would have to stand in front of the class all alone.

Maria wasn't sure she wanted to do this.

She didn't want people to stare at her.

For one thing, her hair was stupid. It was short and straight. Not long and braided like Mary Kate's.

Mary Kate sat next to her. Her braids were really long. She was sucking on the tip of one while she was reading. She had bunny barrettes on her braids.

Maria didn't wear barrettes. Her mother said they didn't look good on her.

Mary Kate had done the January calendar. She had looked great in front of the class. She was lucky. She had all her new teeth. They were the same size.

Maria's teeth were all small, except for her two new front teeth. They were enormous.

Maria wanted bunny rabbit barrettes. Not bunny rabbit teeth.

But maybe she should do the calendar anyway. There were only three chances left. April, May, and June.

"We're not going to do the calendar today," said Mr. Carson.

"Why not?" asked Michael Finn.

"We're having a Do Nothing Day," said Mr. Carson. "So put your books away. Fold your hands on your desk, and keep quiet until lunch."

Maria Lopez couldn't believe her ears. A Do Nothing Day? No reading? No writing? No recess?

What a boring day it would be. But at least now Maria wouldn't have to think about the calendar anymore.

She put her book in her desk and folded her hands.

So did Mary Kate, Rusty, Jane, John, and Lisa.

But not Michael Finn.

He was too smart.

"April Fools," he said. "Am I right?"

Mr. Carson grinned. "You're right," he said. "You can get your books back out of your desks."

Kids laughed. Everyone but Michael had forgotten that April first was April Fools' Day.

Maria grinned.

She wanted to play a trick on someone, too. Maybe she could play one on Mary Kate.

The class started silent reading again.

What do little girl grizzlies wear in their hair?

Bear-ettes.

Maria began to giggle. She thought Mary Kate would like that riddle.

Maybe she and Mary Kate could get to be friends.

Maria giggled again a little louder. She hoped Mary Kate would notice.

It worked.

Mary Kate asked, "What's so funny?"

Maria showed her the riddle.

Mary Kate laughed, too.

"Please be quiet during reading time," said Mr. Carson.

Maria and Mary Kate went back to their books.

Maria felt happy. She was sure she and Mary Kate were going to be friends. Maybe even best friends.

Maria really wanted a best friend.

There was just one problem.

Maria's mother was a college professor. Her college was nearby. She taught in the morning and picked Maria up at school.

Then they went shopping together.

Or to the library.

Or to a museum.

Or to ballet class. They were in a special mother-and-daughter class.

Maria liked her mother.

But she also wanted a friend her age.

She didn't know how to tell that to her mother. Her mother didn't like her to play with other kids.

What sound do grizzlies make when they kiss?

Ouch!

Maria snorted with laughter.

"Shh-h-h!" said Mary Kate. "Stop making so much noise! You're bothering me!"

Maria felt horrible. For a moment she thought she was going to cry.

"April Fools," whispered Mary Kate. "I'm not really mad."

Maria rolled her eyes and laughed. What a relief! She laughed some more. It was fun to be tricked by her new friend.

Suddenly Maria had a good idea.

At lunch Maria sat next to Mary Kate. She waited until Mary Kate was about to drink her milk.

Then Maria yelled, "Watch out for the ants!"

Mary Kate dropped her milk. It spilled all over her dress and her tray.

"April . . . !" Maria started to yell. But she stopped when she saw the look on Mary Kate's face.

Mary Kate wasn't laughing.

"It was a joke," whispered Maria.

"Ha-ha," said Mary Kate angrily.

Maria felt terrible.

She helped Mary Kate wipe up the mess. But she didn't know what else to do.

She hoped she hadn't lost Mary Kate as a friend.

* * *

MILK

That night Maria and her mother ate in a restaurant. Maria ordered fried chicken. It smelled delicious. Maria lifted a leg to her mouth.

"Watch out for the caterpillar!" cried her mother.

Maria dropped her chicken.

"April Fools," said her mother.

Maria couldn't believe it.

This was the third time she had been caught!

And she hadn't played a good trick on anyone yet.

Now it was 6:30 P.M. April Fools' Day was almost over.

"Your April vacation is coming up," said her mom. "How would you like to go to Texas?"

"To see Papá and *Abuelita*?" asked Maria. Abuelita was her grandmother.

"Yes," said her mom.

This was Maria's chance.

She made herself look unhappy. "I don't want to go," she said.

"You don't?" asked her mother. She looked shocked.

"Texas is too hot," said Maria. "And last time I was there I couldn't sleep."

"You couldn't?" Her mother was very upset. "What will we do? I have to go to a conference in Dallas that week. And I thought you could stay in Brownsville."

"April Fools!" said Maria.

Her mother shut her eyes and smiled.

Maria was thrilled twice over. She was thrilled that she had finally played a trick on someone. And thrilled about going to Texas.

It was like having a double-decker ice-cream cone. Which gave Maria another idea.

She took a bite of chicken and made a face.

"This chicken needs ice cream," she said.

"Ice cream?" said her mother. "Are you crazy?"

"April Fools!" shouted Maria.

Chapter 2

The next day at school Mr. Carson asked for calendar volunteers. He had decided to do the calendar on April second. This way there would be no April Fools' Day tricks on it.

Maria looked at Mary Kate. Mary Kate didn't seem mad about the milk anymore.

"Should I do it?" asked Maria.

"Sure!" said Mary Kate. Mary Kate always said "sure" in a cheerful way. She wasn't afraid of anything.

So now Maria *had* to raise her hand. Otherwise Mary Kate would think she was a wimp. Maria could feel her heart thumping under her jersey.

Mr. Carson looked around the room. His eyes landed on Maria.

"Maria Lopez," he said.

Maria's heart stopped thumping for a second. She took a deep breath.

Then she went to the front of the room.

She faced the board and erased March.

As she did so, the rest of the class sang the calendar song. It was to the tune of "Good Night, Ladies."

"Good-bye, March,
Good-bye, March,
Good-bye, March,
See you in a year."

Maria felt important. She washed the board nice and clean.

Then she picked up the chalk and stared at the board. The wet spots were getting smaller and smaller.

Maria waited for someone to tell her what to write.

She could feel everyone staring at her back.

"Friday is Arbor Day," said Mr. Carson.

As neatly as she could, Maria wrote Arbor Day under the square for April fourth. Her hand was shaking a little. But her printing looked okay.

"Does anyone know what we celebrate on Arbor Day?" asked Mr. Carson.

Maria wondered if kids had their hands up. She made herself turn around to see. She kept her lips together so no one would see her rabbit teeth.

She was surprised to see no hands up. Not even Michael Finn seemed to know about Arbor Day.

Maria looked at Mr. Carson. He always wore bow ties. Today his bow tie had little trees on it.

Maria wondered if that was a clue. She thought that Arbor Day might have something to do with trees. But she was afraid to say that.

What if she was completely wrong? Standing in front of the class? Everyone would look at her and laugh.

Maria kept her mouth shut. And her big teeth hidden.

"We celebrate trees," said Mr. Carson.

Now Maria wished she had spoken up. She would have sounded as smart as a teacher.

Michael Finn's hand popped into the air.

"How do we celebrate trees?" he asked.

"It's up to us," said Mr. Carson. "Any ideas?"

Maria had an idea. She thought the class could plant a tree. But she didn't say a word. Again she worried that she would be wrong. And look stupid.

Lots of kids had their hands up now.

"We could make tree paintings," said Rusty.

"And write tree poems," said Lisa.

"We could find out how trees are mathematical," said John.

Maria smiled, keeping her lips together. Mr. Carson loved math. He loved to have kids think up math projects to do.

"Any other ideas?" he asked.

Mary Kate raised her hand. "We could plant a tree in the school yard," she said.

"What a wonderful idea," said Mr. Carson.

"An apple tree," said Rusty.

"For Appleville School!" cried Jane. "That's a great idea, Mary Kate."

Now Maria wished she had said her idea. And she wished Jane had said *her* idea was great.

Still, she was happy for Mary Kate.

Maria wrote "Plant an apple tree" under April fourth.

Her hand wasn't shaking anymore. She felt like a real teacher.

When she went back to her seat, she

said, "Good idea," to Mary Kate in a teacher kind of way.

Mr. Carson asked the kids to pick partners for Arbor Day. After the tree was planted the partners would tell how trees were mathematical.

Did Maria dare to ask Mary Kate to be her partner?

Yes.

Slowly she reached out and touched Mary Kate's arm. "Do you want to be my partner?" she whispered.

"Sure!" said Mary Kate.

Maria's heart felt like sunshine after rain. "Do you have any ideas?" she asked.

"Come over to my house after school," said Mary Kate. "We can make a list of them."

"I can't," said Maria. "I have to go to ballet."

"How about tomorrow?" asked Mary Kate.

"I'm going to the library," said Maria.

Mary Kate frowned. "Thursday? That's the last day we can work on the report. Arbor Day is Friday."

"I think I'm free," said Maria. "But I have to check with my mother."

"Call me when you find out," said Mary Kate. She wrote her phone number on a slip of paper and gave it to Maria.

Maria put it in her back pocket. She felt proud to have Mary Kate's number.

But she was worried about her mother. What if her mother wouldn't let her go to Mary Kate's house?

Chapter 3

Maria lay in bed and listened to her mom read. Dr. Lopez was reading their favorite storybook, *Many Moons,* by James Thurber.

It was about a princess who was sick and needed the moon to get better. The king didn't know how to get the moon. So he was very upset.

Maria's mother and Maria had mother-and-daughter polka dot nightgowns. The dots were like big white moons.

Maria wondered if Princess Lenore would have settled for a polka dot nightgown.

All Maria wanted was a best friend.

"Can I go to Mary Kate's house on Thursday?" she asked.

"We're going to the hairdresser," said Dr. Lopez.

Maria's mother wasn't a doctor's office doctor. She was a college doctor. If you studied hard and long enough, people called you doctor. Maria's mother was a doctor of history.

"Mary Kate and I have to do a report together," said Maria. "She asked me to go to her house to work on it."

"But I don't know Mary Kate," said her mother. "I don't know her family, either. It will make me nervous if you go there."

Maria knew why her mother was nervous. Ever since her mother and father had been divorced, her mother was nervous. She was always afraid something bad would happen to Maria.

But Maria didn't think anything bad would happen to her. So she said, "What about this? I'll invite Mary Kate to come to our house on Thursday. You and I can go to the hairdresser on Friday."

Dr. Lopez didn't look happy, but she agreed.

She was, after all, a nice mom. But a worried one, too.

The next morning Maria and her mom left for school.

Maria saw Mary Kate across the street and waved. Mary Kate waved back.

"That's Mary Kate!" said Maria. "Should I ask her now about Thursday?"

"Okay," said her mother. "But hurry. I have to teach an early class."

But Maria grew scared. What if Mary Kate didn't like her mother? What if Mary Kate said no?

"I'll ask her later," said Maria.

"Okay," said her mother. "Who are those other kids?"

"Jane and Fizz Eddie Fox," said Maria.

"What kind of a name is Fizz Eddie?" asked her mother.

"He's called that because he's good at phys ed," said Maria.

"Don't those kids need a grown-up to walk with them?" asked her mother.

"Fizz Eddie's in junior high," said Maria.

"I see," said her mother.

But Maria could tell she didn't see at all.

Dr. Lopez didn't see how any parent would let a child walk to school without a grown-up.

Which was too bad because Maria would have loved to walk to school with Mary Kate, Jane, and Fizz Eddie.

If they didn't ever walk to school together, how could she and Mary Kate get to be best friends?

Maybe Mary Kate was already best friends with Jane.

Maria didn't know very much about Mary Kate.

When Maria went into her classroom, she saw Mary Kate sitting alone at her desk.

It was the perfect moment to ask her about Thursday.

But again Maria felt too worried. What if Mary Kate said she was going to Jane's house?

Maria decided to wait until recess. She would see if Mary Kate played with Jane.

But at recess Mary Kate was playing jacks with Sharon. Sharon was in fourth grade. She had pink high-top sneakers, pink earrings, and pink nail polish.

Maybe Sharon was Mary Kate's best friend.

She sure was good at jacks. She was beating Mary Kate by a mile.

Maria walked over. She stood next to the girls and watched.

Sharon won. "Want to play again?" she asked.

"Sure!" said Mary Kate.

Nobody said a word to Maria.

If she wanted them to notice her, she would have to speak up.

Mary Kate picked up the jacks. She was just about to throw them when Maria said, "Mary Kate?"

Mary Kate didn't answer. She threw the jacks.

"Mary Kate?" said Maria, louder.

Sharon looked up. "Do you mean Mountain Dew?" she asked. Then she began to giggle.

Maria looked at Mary Kate. "What is

Sharon talking about?" she asked.

"Do you mean Shasta?" asked Mary Kate. She was giggling, too.

The two girls were hysterical. Mary Kate was laughing so hard she dropped the jacks.

Maria turned away. Her face felt hot. She was very confused. Was this an April Fools' joke? On April third? She didn't think so.

Tears filled her eyes. Before they could drop down her cheeks, Maria ran into the school.

Mr. Carson was sitting at his desk. Maria ran past him. She sat at her desk and put her head down. She tried not to make a sound even though she was crying.

But Mr. Carson knew something was wrong.

"What's the trouble?" he asked.

"Nothing," said Maria. She wiped her eyes with her sleeve.

"You sure?" asked Mr. Carson. He came over and sat in Mary Kate's seat.

Maria nodded.

"Well, all right," said Mr. Carson. "But if you have a problem, you can always tell me about it. Now or later."

Mr. Carson went back to his desk.

Maria got out her leaf drawings. She tried to concentrate on them.

She had looked up information on leaves in a book. One thing she learned was that leaves have jagged edges called teeth.

Maria drew a big leaf with teeth. She was going to suggest to Mary Kate that they count the teeth on leaves for their report.

Mary Kate came in from recess. She sat down in her seat and started drawing, too.

Maria watched her out of the corner of her eyes.

Mary Kate drew a can of soda. It said Shasta on it. Then she drew another can. It said Mountain Dew.

She drew two eyes and a smile on each can. The eyes had curly eyelashes.

Then she drew dresses under the cans. The dresses had full skirts and puffy sleeves.

Maria drew a face on her leaf. She drew a dress under it, too. That gave her an idea.

"I have an idea," she said to Mary Kate. "We could draw leaf puppets for our project."

Mary Kate frowned. "They're not mathematical," she said. "Anyway, you copied my soda can girls. Sharon and I have a Soda Can Club."

Maria felt her heart start to pound. The club sounded wonderful. But scary.

"Can I be in it?" she asked. Please say yes, she said to herself. Please, please, please!

"That depends," said Mary Kate. "You have to have a soda pop name that begins with the same letter as your name. For example, Sharon is Shasta. And I'm Mountain Dew. Who could you be?"

"Can I be Mountain Dew, too?" asked Maria.

"No," said Mary Kate. She shook her head so hard her braids flew into the air. "M is taken. I'm the only Mountain Dew in the world."

Maria's heart was pounding even more. She tried to think of another M soda.

Coca-Cola.

Pepsi.

Dr Pepper.

Orangina.

Root beer.

Not one began with M.

All she could think of was maple syrup. Mayonnaise. Mushrooms. Margarine.

She could never be in the Soda Can Club.

Maria felt tears coming into her eyes again. But she didn't want to cry in front of Mary Kate.

So she said, "That's stupid."

She shrugged her shoulders and sighed. She acted as if Mary Kate were very childish.

And she made herself act very grown-up.

She went back to her leaf drawing. She added monster teeth to the mouth. And big mean eyebrows.

Maybe she would start a club of her own.

A leaf club.

But who would she get to be in it?

The only person she could think of was her mother.

Chapter 4

"Did you ask that girl over Thursday?" said Dr. Lopez at supper. She and Maria were eating macaroni and cheese.

"No," said Maria. "And I don't want to anymore. I'm going to do my report myself."

But Maria still had Mary Kate's phone number. And she was supposed to call her.

"Then we'll go to the hairdresser's Thursday," said her mother. "On Friday we'll start shopping for summer clothes."

"It's only April," said Maria.

Her mother smiled. "April in Texas is very hot."

"Texas!" said Maria. "I almost forgot we were going there."

Thinking about Texas cheered her up.

But she still had to call Mary Kate.

After supper Dr. Lopez did the dishes.

Maria sat by the phone in her mother's bedroom.

She fished Mary Kate's phone number out of her back pocket.

She started to dial, then stopped.

She didn't know what to say.

"Hello, Mountain Dew?" She wouldn't start that way. That was for sure.

She could say, "Hello, Mary Kate? I'm sorry I can't come Thursday. I'm doing my report alone. Thank you very much. Good-bye." Then she would hang up.

Yes, that was it.

Maria dialed.

A little kid picked up and said, "Hello?"

Maria guessed it was Joey, Mary Kate's little brother.

"Hello," she said. "Is Mary Kate there?"

"Yes," said Joey.

Maria could hear him breathing.

"Can I talk to her?" she asked.

"Yes," said Joey.

Maria could still hear him breathing.

"Will you go get her?" asked Maria.

"Yes," said Joey.

But Maria could *still* hear him breathing.

"Go and tell her the phone is for her," said Maria.

"Okay," said Joey.

But Maria could *STILL* hear him breathing.

"GO GET YOUR SISTER!" screamed Maria.

"Who are you talking to?" asked Dr. Lopez. She had just come into the room.

Maria slammed down the phone. "No one," she said.

"But I heard you screaming," said her mother.

"I was just pretending," said Maria.

"Oh, good," said her mom. "You had me worried for a minute."

Maria sighed.

She would have to tell Mary Kate the next day.

Maria and her mom went into the dining room.

Dr. Lopez opened her briefcase. She started correcting papers on the table.

Maria opened her drawer. She had a special drawer in the table for art supplies.

She started drawing leaves. She and her mother worked quietly together.

They did this most evenings. They called it their "Office Time."

Maria made ten pictures of ten different leaves. Without faces. And without dresses.

She counted the teeth on each leaf and wrote the number in the corner. She labeled each leaf correctly.

Then she made a cover for her report.

It had big green letters that said, *LEAF TEETH*.

Under the title she wrote, *By Maria Lopez*.

She stapled her report together. It looked great. She showed it to her mother.

"Beautiful," said her mother. "Maybe you will be a doctor of botany someday."

"What's botany?" asked Maria.

"The study of plants," said her mother.

Maria thought about that.

"Is there such a thing as being a doctor of the way people act?" she asked.

"What do you mean?" said her mother.

"Some leaves have teeth, and some don't," said Maria. "People can study that, right? Well, some people are nice, and some aren't. Can you study that, too?"

Her mother thought about it. "You can be a doctor of psychology," she said. "That's the study of how people think and feel. Or you could be a doctor of sociology. That's the study of how people act in groups."

"Do doctors of sociology study clubs?" asked Maria.

"Yes," said her mother. "I think they do."

"Then that's what I'm going to be," said Maria. "A doctor of sociology."

"Are you interested in clubs?" said her mother.

"Sort of," said Maria. She didn't want to say any more. She didn't want to tell her mother about the Soda Can Club.

Chapter 5

The next day Maria brought her report to school. She put it on her desk and hoped Mary Kate would see it.

She did.

"What's that?" she asked.

"My report," said Maria.

"I thought we were supposed to do it together," said Mary Kate.

"I tried calling you," said Maria. "But your brother wouldn't put down the phone and get you."

"That little pain!" said Mary Kate. "You have no idea how much trouble he is."

She looked at the report again. "Can I at least see it?" she asked.

"I guess so," said Maria.

Mary Kate turned the pages. "It's great," she said. "You did a good job."

Maria felt happy to hear those words.

"Can I still do it with you?" asked Mary Kate. "I could add some pages. And you could add my name on the front."

"I guess," said Maria.

"Oh, thank you!" said Mary Kate. She reached over and gave Maria a hug.

Maria was very mixed up.

Maybe Mary Kate wasn't so bad. And maybe she didn't like Shasta anymore. Maybe the stupid Soda Can Club was a thing of the past.

Maria grinned and hugged Mary Kate back.

Arbor Day was rainy.

"Do we still have to go out?" asked Michael.

"Of course," said Mr. Carson. "Rain is good for trees. It makes perfect sense to have rain on Arbor Day."

Everyone in the elementary school put on their rain gear and went outside.

Each class stood together around a big circle.

In the middle of the circle was Fizz Eddie with a shovel. He had volunteered to dig the hole.

"Welcome to Arbor Day," he said.

Two kindergartners in yellow raincoats came forward. They were carrying a little pine tree. They put it in the hole.

Everyone sang to the tune of "Happy Birthday."

"Happy Arbor Day to you,
Happy Arbor Day to you,
Happy Arbor Day, Happy Arbor Day,
Happy Arbor Day to you."

Then Mr. Carson stepped forward. "My class will now tell you how trees are mathematical," he said.

Maria and Mary Kate stepped forward.

Mary Kate held the umbrella while Maria read.

"Did you know that leaves can have teeth? Teeth are the jagged edges of leaves. Some teeth are big. Some are small."

Then Maria held the umbrella while Mary Kate read.

"We found nine big teeth and seven small teeth on an oak leaf. We found five big teeth and 121 small teeth on a Japanese maple leaf."

Everyone clapped. Maria and Mary Kate walked back to their group.

Maria was so happy she hardly listened to the other reports. But she did learn that the heaviest tree weighs 6,000 tons.

And that a single oak tree can grow 50,000 acorns.

Wow! That was amazing.

But nothing was so amazing as her new friendship with Mary Kate.

They had done a great report together. And now they were standing together like true best friends.

All of a sudden Sharon stepped into the middle of the circle.

She was wearing a bright green raincoat. Her rain hat had red and yellow flowers on it.

"She looks like a flower," whispered Maria.

"I know," said Mary Kate. "Isn't she beautiful?"

Maria couldn't believe her ears. Did Mary Kate still like Sharon? She had to find out.

"Do you two still have that club?" she whispered.

"Of course we do," said Mary Kate. "We call it the Best Friends Soda Can Club."

HOW CAN YOU HAVE A BEST

FRIENDS CLUB WITHOUT ME? Maria wanted to scream.

But she didn't.

She didn't say a word.

But that night she ripped up their report and threw it away.

Chapter 6

Maria couldn't wait for April vacation. She wanted to get as far away as possible from Mary Kate Adams. And her stupid friend Sharon. And their stupid Soda Can Club.

Maria noticed the blue sky on the way to the airport.

"It's a good day for flying," she said, to cheer her mother up. Maria knew her mother was nervous about flying.

But Maria wasn't nervous at all. She had flown to Texas five times before. She liked to fly.

The flight attendant gave her a coloring book and a little airplane pin.

"Can my mother have a present, too?" asked Maria.

The flight attendant smiled down at her. She thought Maria was cute.

But Maria wasn't trying to be cute. She was serious. The attendants should give grown-ups presents, too. Maybe that would make them feel better, thought Maria.

Maria fastened her seat belt and looked out the window. She saw little men driving carts filled with suitcases. They loaded the suitcases onto the plane. Then they drove away.

Maria examined her coloring book. It showed pictures of different kinds of planes.

Maria colored the first plane red.

The plane began to move. Dr. Lopez grabbed Maria's hand.

"Here we go!" said Maria.

She heard a whooshing sound. The little men in the carts became smaller and smaller.

"We're flying!" she said. She felt like she was on a roller coaster. Only instead of going up and down, she kept going straight.

I bet Mary Kate never did this, Maria thought. She vowed not to write her a postcard from Texas.

Lunch on the plane was macaroni and cheese. The flight attendant asked her what she wanted to drink.

"What kind of sodas do you have?" asked Maria. Maybe the lady would name an M soda she hadn't thought of.

"Mountain Dew, Shasta . . . "

"Forget it," said Maria. "I'll have milk."

The movie was *Ghostbusters*. Maria had seen it before, but she liked seeing it again.

After the movie she looked out the window. She saw wispy clouds below the plane. Under the clouds were little highways and land.

She felt as if she could see the whole world. That made her think of a song she had learned in school.

It was called "He's Got the Whole World in His Hands." Maria hummed it quietly to herself and fell asleep.

She forgot all about the Soda Can Club.

Ding! The seat-belt bell rang in the cabin. The flight attendant said the plane was getting ready to land.

Maria's mother grabbed her hand. "Don't worry, Mom," said Maria.

She looked out the window. The Brownsville airport was coming closer.

Bump! The plane hit the ground. Her mother squeezed her hand.

Maria squeezed back.

"We're here!" she said. She heard a big

whooshing sound. That was the jet engines that slowed the plane down.

The plane drove slowly up to the passenger terminal. Maria looked out the window. She saw people waving from the window of the terminal.

"There's Papá!" she cried. "And Abuelita!"

Dr. Lopez put on lipstick and brushed her hair.

Then she brushed Maria's hair.

Everyone else was leaving the plane.

"Come on, Mom," said Maria. "Let's go!"

Her mother took a deep breath. "Okay," she said.

As they left the plane, the pilot came out of the cockpit. He shook hands with Maria and asked her if she had enjoyed the trip.

"I did, but my mother didn't," said Maria.

The pilot laughed. He walked off the plane with them.

I bet Mary Kate never met a pilot, Maria said to herself.

Then she saw her father. Maria ran into his open arms.

She felt his tickly mustache as he gave her a kiss on the cheek.

Then Maria hugged Abuelita. Abuelita was the softest person in the world.

Out of the corner of her eyes, Maria watched her mother and her father. They were shaking hands.

Maria had never seen them kiss. She couldn't remember when her father had lived with them. To her it seemed that he had always lived with Abuelita.

And he always shook her mother's hand.

Sometimes Maria wished her mother and father would get in bed and kiss like the Cosbys on television.

But maybe that would be weird. The fact was, her mom and dad shook hands, and that was that. Maria was used to it.

Now came the hard part. Saying good-bye to her mother. Dr. Lopez was going to take a plane to Dallas in a few minutes.

Maria and her mother hugged each other tightly.

"I'll be back Sunday," said Dr. Lopez. "Have a wonderful time!"

"I will," said Maria. She felt a lump in her throat, so she hugged her mother again.

"Don't forget to brush your teeth!" said her mother.

"I won't!" said Maria. She smiled as bravely as she could to cheer up her mom.

Her mother ran down the corridor. She turned around twice to wave, and then she was gone.

Maria walked through the airport with

Papá and Abuelita. They passed many shops.

Mexican music was playing in one of them. In the window was a little Mexican doll. She had on high heels, a full skirt, a pink shawl, and a big straw hat.

"What a sad, sad doll," said Papá.

"What do you mean?" said Maria. "She has a big smile on her face."

"How can a doll be happy with no one to take care of her?" said Papá. "She probably doesn't even have a name."

"I would name her Conchita," said Maria. That was her mother's first name.

Papá took out his wallet and went into the store. In a few minutes Maria had Conchita in her arms.

"Muchas gracias," she said shyly.

Her father looked very happy. He liked Maria to speak Spanish.

He picked Maria and Conchita up and

stood in front of an orange juice stand. Abuelita took their picture with a flash camera.

Then Papá bought everyone a glass of orange juice. "Fresh squeezed from Texas oranges," he said. *"Muy bueno."*

They drove out of the airport in Papa's yellow jeep. They rode past orange orchards and grapefruit orchards. Above them was the big Texas sky.

Maria saw a tiny plane in the sky. Was it her mother's? Maria felt bad that her mother didn't have anyone to hold hands with.

They drove on an expressway and then on smaller roads. They went past a mall and turned down a street that Maria began to remember.

Down the next street she could see Abuelita's brick house. It had palm trees and flower gardens in the front yard.

On the front steps sat two little girls.

"That's Dalia and Juanita," said Maria's father. "They're new to the neighborhood. We told them you were coming. They've been waiting for you."

The two girls were very shy. They were sewing dolls' clothes. Actually they weren't really sewing. Just cutting out scarves and ponchos.

Maria didn't see any dolls. She showed the girls her new doll, Conchita. "Who are your scarves and ponchos for?" she asked.

"For the little old man," said the oldest girl. "Want to help us?"

Maria said yes. She knew what they were talking about.

The little old man was a small cactus in her grandmother's garden. Abuelita called him *Viejito*, or "little old man." Once her grandmother had put a pair of sunglasses on him. "To protect him from the sun," she had said.

Maria's father bent down and kissed Maria good-bye. "I've got to go back to the bank," he said. "But tomorrow I'm off. I'll take you and your new friends to the beach."

Maria was excited to hear that. Going to the beach was one of her favorite things to do in Texas.

She waved good-bye to her father. Then she picked up the cloth and scissors. "I think I'll make Viejito a hat," she said.

"My sister only knows how to make a scarf," said Dalia. "She's only five. But I can make a poncho. I'm six. How old are you?"

"Almost nine," said Maria.

Really she was only eight and a half. But eight and a half could be rounded off to nine. Mr. Carson had taught her that.

Maria cut out a round piece of red cloth. The two younger girls watched closely.

Maria picked up a needle and a piece

of thread. She licked the thread and stuck the point through the hole in the needle.

"You can do that?" asked Dalia.

"Sure!" said Maria. She said it in the cheerful way Mary Kate did. Carefully she stitched around the circle's edge.

Dalia and Juanita watched her as if she were a movie star.

Maria pulled the thread and said, *"¡Iya!"* The cloth gathered up into a little cap with a ruffled edge.

Maria tied a big knot in her thread. Then she put the hat on Viejito.

"That's amazing," said Dalia.

Abuelita came out with drinks and cookies. She sat down to sew, too. She made Viejito a blue skirt.

"A skirt?" said Maria. "For an old man?"

"How are you going to put pants on a cactus?" said Abuelita.

Everyone laughed. A skirt it would have to be.

Dalia made a new poncho. Juanita made a new scarf.

Then they put all the clothes on Viejito. He looked as if he were dressed for snowy weather in New Jersey.

Thinking of New Jersey made Maria think of Mary Kate again. She was probably getting beaten by Sharon at jacks.

Maria was glad she was in Texas with Dalia and Juanita.

Dalia could be Diet Pepsi.

But Juanita?

Maria began to think. Jam. Jelly. Jell-O. Nope. She couldn't think of one soda that began with J.

Not that it mattered, of course.

Maria was *not* going to start a Texas Soda Can Club.

Because if she did, she would have to be Mountain Dew.

And Mountain Dew was already taken.

Oh sure, she could take it, too. Mary Kate would never know.

But what would be the point of starting the club if she couldn't tell Mary Kate about it?

Chapter 7

The next day Maria's father drove Maria, Dalia, and Juanita to the beach.

Maria sat up front with her father. Mexican music played on the radio. Papá knew some of the songs by heart.

Maria liked to hear her father sing. Even if she didn't understand all the Spanish words.

That was one thing she knew her parents argued about. Maria's father wanted her mother to talk to her in Spanish at home.

But Maria's mother didn't want to do that. So Maria knew only a little Spanish.

Dalia and Juanita spoke both Spanish and English.

Maybe if Maria learned Spanish, her parents would get married again. Then they would kiss and hug like the Cosbys.

"Buenos días, Don Miguel," she said aloud. That's what the man had said to her father at the gas station.

Her father laughed. *"Buenos días, Hijita!"* he said.

Maria smiled. She knew that meant, "Good day, Little Daughter!"

At the beach she played in the water with her father and the girls. Then her father went to sunbathe.

The girls collected shells.

Maria found some really good ones. So did Diet Pepsi.

Maria surprised herself by thinking of the soda can name again. Why did she keep doing that? The truth was, she really wanted to start a Soda Can Club.

Juanita filled her pail with ugly broken shells.

"That's because she's only five," whispered Diet Pepsi. "She's too young to know the difference."

Suddenly Maria had an idea. Her father had called her Hijita.

Hijita began with an H.

H for Hires Root Beer.

Maria was walking next to Dalia. Juanita had run ahead.

"Dalia," said Maria. "Let's have a special club. To belong you have to have a soda pop name that begins with the same letter as your name. Or nickname. For example, my nickname is Hijita. So my secret name is Hires Root Beer. Yours is Diet Pepsi."

Diet Pepsi looked a little confused. "What's the club for?" she asked.

"For best friends," said Hires. "But your sister can't belong. Her name begins with

J. And there's no soda that begins with the letter J."

Diet Pepsi's eyes lit up. "And besides, her shells are all junky," she said.

"I know," agreed Hires. "They're gross. Let's not mix ours with hers."

Juanita was running back down the beach. She was coming right up to them. "Dalia, Dalia!" she cried. "Look what I found!"

Juanita had a little gold shell with no holes in it.

Maria almost wanted to say, "Great, Juanita!" But she didn't. Instead she said, "Do you mean Diet Pepsi?"

Juanita looked confused. "What?" she said.

Maria started to laugh.

"Why is Maria laughing at me?" Juanita asked her sister.

"Don't you mean Hires Root Beer?" asked Dalia.

Dalia burst into laughter and fell on the

ground. Maria fell down next to her. They rolled in the sand, howling.

Maria held her stomach and laughed as hard as she could. "Ha, ha, HA!" she laughed. She laughed louder than she had ever laughed in her whole life.

But deep down inside she knew she was faking.

After a while she stopped.

And when she stopped, Dalia stopped, too.

The two girls looked up at Juanita. She was still holding her shell.

Her eyes were round and rimmed with tears.

"Don't you like my shell?" she asked.

Maria sat up and looked at the little gold shell. It was no bigger than her thumbnail. But to Juanita it was the most beautiful shell in the whole wide world.

Maria swallowed. "It's great," she said.

"It's really gold," whispered Juanita.

Maria looked at Dalia. Dalia shrugged. Then she said, "It's the best shell we found all day."

Juanita shut her fist around her treasure and smiled from ear to ear.

Maria smiled, too.

Right then and there, she learned something about herself.

She wasn't the type for secret clubs. Secret clubs with secret names were mean.

And she wasn't mean.

Shy, maybe.

But not mean.

And, come to think of it, not really that shy.

For example, she wasn't too shy to talk to the airplane pilot.

And she wasn't too shy to try to learn Spanish.

And she wasn't too shy to make friends with Dalia and Juanita.

The only people she felt *really* shy with were girls who started secret clubs.

Figuring that out made Maria feel much better. She ran into the water and splashed like a fish.

The happiest fish in the Gulf of Mexico.

Chapter 8

"How was your vacation?" asked Mr. Carson.

Maria had come to school early that day. No one else was there yet. *"Muy bueno,"* she said. "Remember that day I came in crying from recess? And I wouldn't tell you what was the matter?"

"Yes," said Mr. Carson.

"I figured out what was wrong," said Maria. "And now it doesn't bother me anymore."

"Good," said Mr. Carson. "Do you want to tell me about it?"

Maria didn't know what to say. On one hand, she did. On the other hand, she didn't.

"You don't have to," said Mr. Carson. He smiled. He had a nice warm smile that made Maria feel good.

He also had a tan and a brand new bow tie. It had raindrops on it.

"For April?" said Maria.

"For April," said Mr. Carson. They both looked out the window.

It was pouring.

"In Brownsville, Texas, it's not like this," said Maria.

"Nor in Miami, Florida," said Mr. Carson.

"Is that where you went?" asked Maria.

Mr. Carson nodded.

Then they both grinned. Without saying so exactly, they had something in common.

They had both been somewhere nice and sunny. And they missed it.

Vacation was over.

Just then Mary Kate came into the room.

"My shoes are all wet!" she said.

"So are mine," said Maria.

"So are mine," said Mr. Carson. "How was your vacation?"

"It was okay," said Mary Kate. "I didn't do much."

"What did you do?" asked Maria.

"I played with Jane and Lisa," said Mary Kate. "I went to the movies. I got a new Nintendo game, and I watched TV."

Maria and Mary Kate walked to their seats.

"Did you play with Sharon?" asked Maria.

Mary Kate wrinkled her nose and made an ugly face. "Sharon has a new friend in fourth grade. Her name is Beth. Every time I called Sharon, she said she had already been invited to play with Beth."

"I made some new friends in Texas," said Maria. "We went to the beach."

"You're lucky," said Mary Kate.

"I found some neat shells," said Maria.

"You want to come over to my house to see them?"

"Sure," said Mary Kate.

"Here," said Maria. "I'll give you my number."

Maria wrote her phone number on a piece of paper and gave it to Mary Kate.

"Thanks," said Mary Kate. She put it in her back pocket and gave Maria a grateful smile.

Then she said, "Remember that riddle book you had? Can I borrow it?"

"Sure!" said Maria.

"Are there any more like it?" asked Mary Kate.

"Sure!" said Maria. "There's *Buggy Riddles* and *Fishy Riddles* and *Snakey Riddles*. They're all at the town library!"

Mary Kate frowned. "I've never been there," she said.

That night the phone rang during "Office Time."

Maria ran to get it.

It was Mary Kate. "Want to make a play date?" she asked.

"Yes," said Maria. "Hold on a minute."

Maria put the phone down and went over to her mother. "That's Mary Kate Adams," she said. "She wants to play with me. Can we invite her to come to the library tomorrow? I think she'd like to go. She needs a little excitement in her life."

Dr. Lopez smiled and got up. "Okay," she said. "Let me talk to her mother, and we'll see what we can arrange."

And that was the beginning of a real friendship that lasted for a long, long time.

It wasn't a club. And it never needed to be one.

About the Author

"I like writing about children and their families," says author Jean Marzollo. "Children are never boring. Whenever I get stuck for an idea, I visit a classroom and talk to the kids. They give me millions of ideas and all I have to do is choose the right one.

"I also like writing about schools and neighborhoods, which are like great big families. People who go to school together and live together learn a lot from each other. They learn to respect each other's differences. Some of my best friends today are people I grew up and went to school with.

"I remember everything about elementary school–my teacher's names, the lamp with painted roses on it that we gave the teacher when she got married, who cried and why on the playground, and how to make fish with fingerpaint.

"When I write the stories for *39 Kids on the Block,* I draw on my childhood memories and my experiences in schools today. I also live with my two teenage sons and husband in Cold Spring, New York, a community with strong values and lots of stories."

Jean Marzollo has written many picture books, easy-to-read books, and novels for children. She has also written books about children for parents and teachers, and articles in *Parents Magazine.*

About the Illustrator

"Jean Marzollo and I have been the best of friends for more than 20 years and we have also worked together on many books," says illustrator Irene Trivas. "She writes about kids, I draw them.

"Once upon a time we both lived in New York and learned all about living in the city. Then we moved away. I went off to Vermont and had to learn how to live in the country. But the kids we met were the same everywhere: complicated, funny, silly, serious, and more imaginative than any grown-up can ever be."

Irene Trivas has illustrated a number of picture books and easy-to-read books for children. She has also written and illustrated her own book, *Emma's Christmas: An Old Song* (Orchard).

More fun with
39 Kids on the Block
Look for #5!

Chicken Pox Strikes Again

Some kids live with one or two grown-ups. But John lives with three. He's surrounded!

And Grampa Beane is mean! He hates everything. And he's always telling John what to do.

Next week Grampa Beane is coming to school. John can just see it. Grampa will embarrass him in front of everyone!

Here are some other books about the **39 Kids on the Block:**

#1 *The Green Ghost of Appleville*
Poor Rusty Morelli. He just moved into a haunted house. Should Mary Kate help him? Or should she just stay away?

#2 *The Best Present Ever*
Each of the 39 Kids on the Block wants the best present ever. Who will get what they want? Who will get what they don't want?

#3 *Roses Are Pink and You Stink!*
Michael Finn is angry. Everyone laughed at him. But Michael has an idea — and they'll be sorry!

#5 *Chicken Pox Strikes Again*
Grampa Beane is so mean. And he's coming to John's school! Maybe, if he's lucky, John won't be there. May he'll get the chicken pox!